Noah the Narwhal

A Tale of Downs and Ups

by Judith Klausner

Illustrated by Sarah Gould

For my mom and dad, for...everything...over the last three decades (and the next many, on speculation). —J. K.

For my grandmother, Queen of the Sharks, for her support and gumption. Never give up. —S.G.

With grateful thanks to Caroline Jalfin—the godmother of Noah the Narwhal—for her passionate commitment to helping to make this book a reality.

Noah the Narwhal: A Tale of Downs and Ups

Dancing Mantis Press

Printed in the United States of America

ISBN 978-0-9990084-2-3

Dancing Mantis Press
DancingMantisPress@gmail.com
www.DancingMantisPress.com

Narwhals

Narwhals are small Arctic whales. They are probably most well known for their unicorn-like "horn" or tusk, which is found on all male narwhals and 15% of female narwhals. All of the narwhals in this story have tusks because we think it's more fun that way.

Narwhals use many different sounds to navigate, communicate, and find food. These include clicks, whistles, knocks, trumpeting, and even a noise like a squeaking door!

On Monday,
Noah the narwhal
woke up feeling fine.

He brushed his twirling horn until it gleamed,
scarfed down a delicious breakfast of cod,
and swam off to work humming the popular tune
"Click Whistle Click."

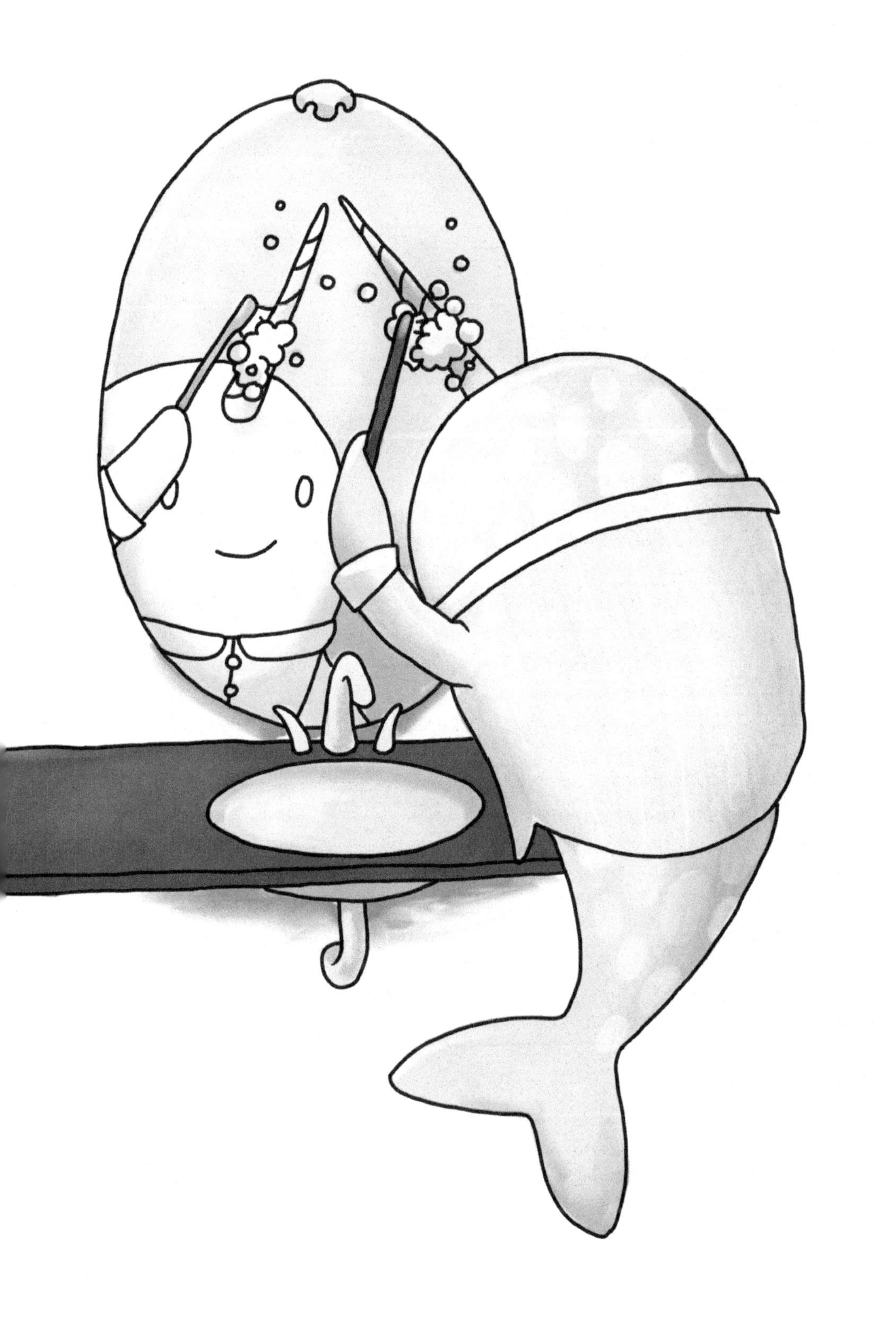

SQUID

At lunch, Noah's friend Nikki asked if he'd like to see a movie.

"*Revenge of the Squid* is showing tomorrow," she said.

"I'll come by and pick you up at six o'clock!"

Noah ate a tasty dinner of shrimp

and went to sleep excited about the next day.

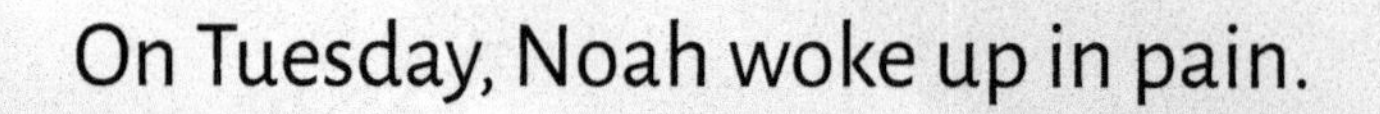

On Tuesday, Noah woke up in pain.

He felt like his horn was growing into his head

instead of out of it.

“Not again,” moaned Noah

as he hid his head under the blanket.

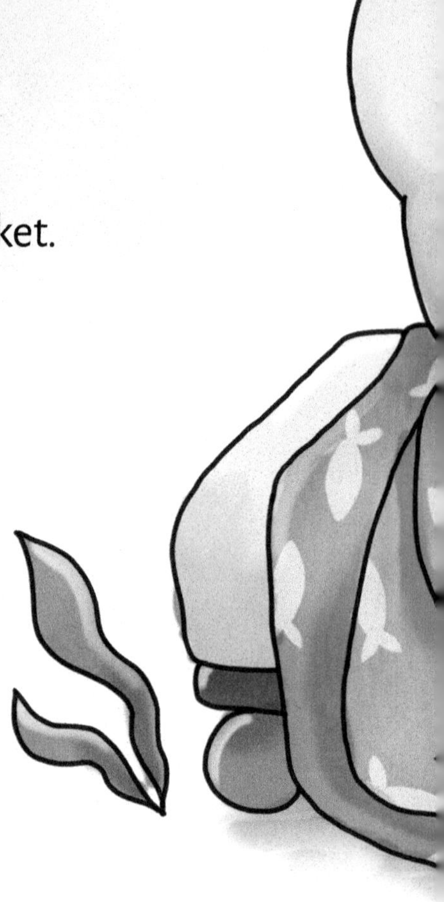

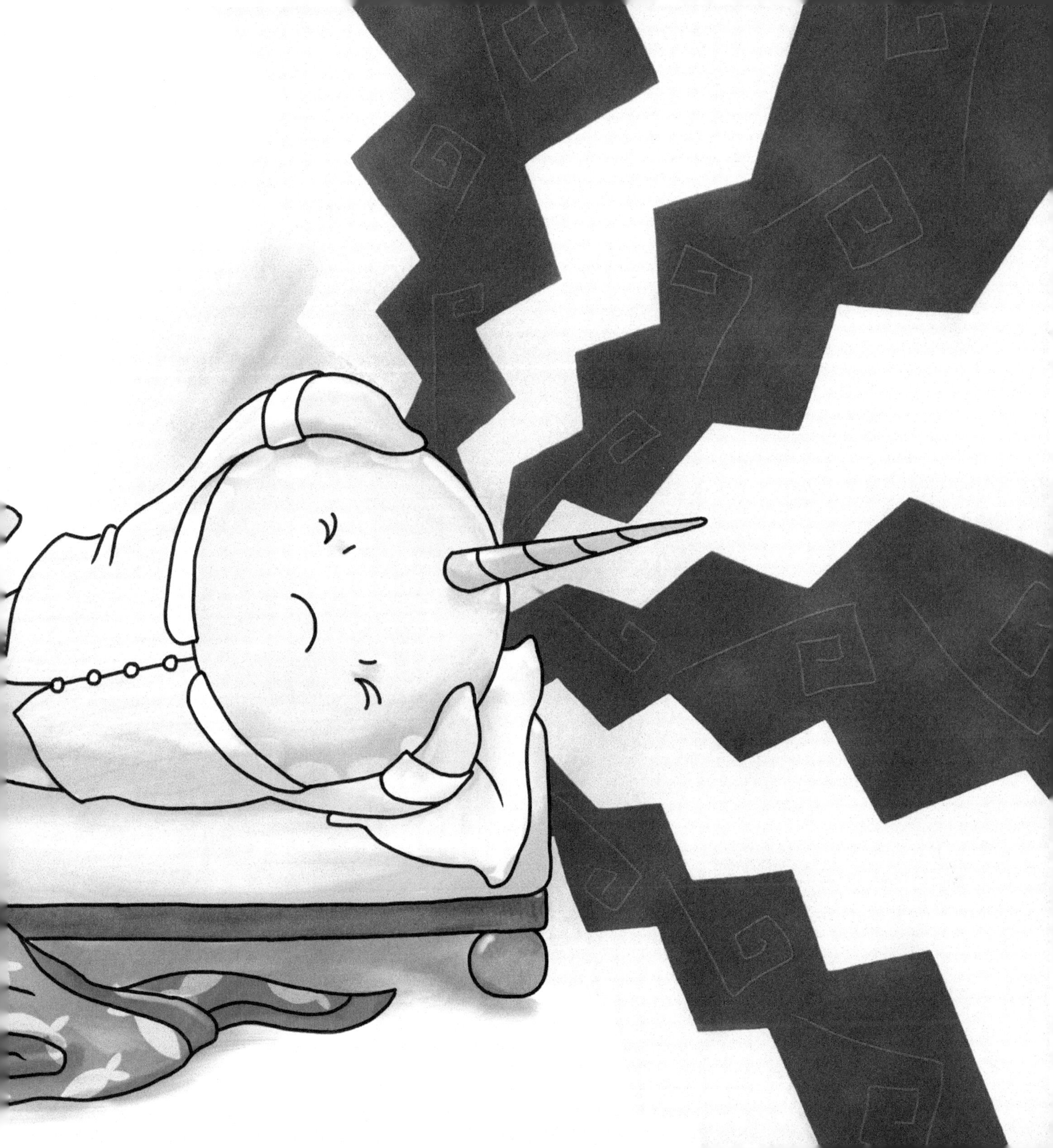

Noah called his boss Norbert

to say he couldn't make it in to work.

“You were feeling fine yesterday,” said Norbert.

“Today is not yesterday,” said Noah,

and he went back to sleep.

“Click click whistle click!”

said his friend Nikki

as she arrived at the door.

Noah winced.

“Not so much ‘whistle’ today, please,” he begged.

“My head feels like it's full of sea urchins.”

“You don't look any different than yesterday,” said Nikki.

“Today is not yesterday,” said Noah,

and went back to sleep, feeling sad.

That night, Noah was woken up again

by a phone call from his sister, Nina.

"I'm sorry, Nina," said Noah, "I can't talk right now."

“But when I called yesterday, you said to call back today,”

she said, sounding upset.

“Today is not yesterday,” said Noah, and he tried not to cry.

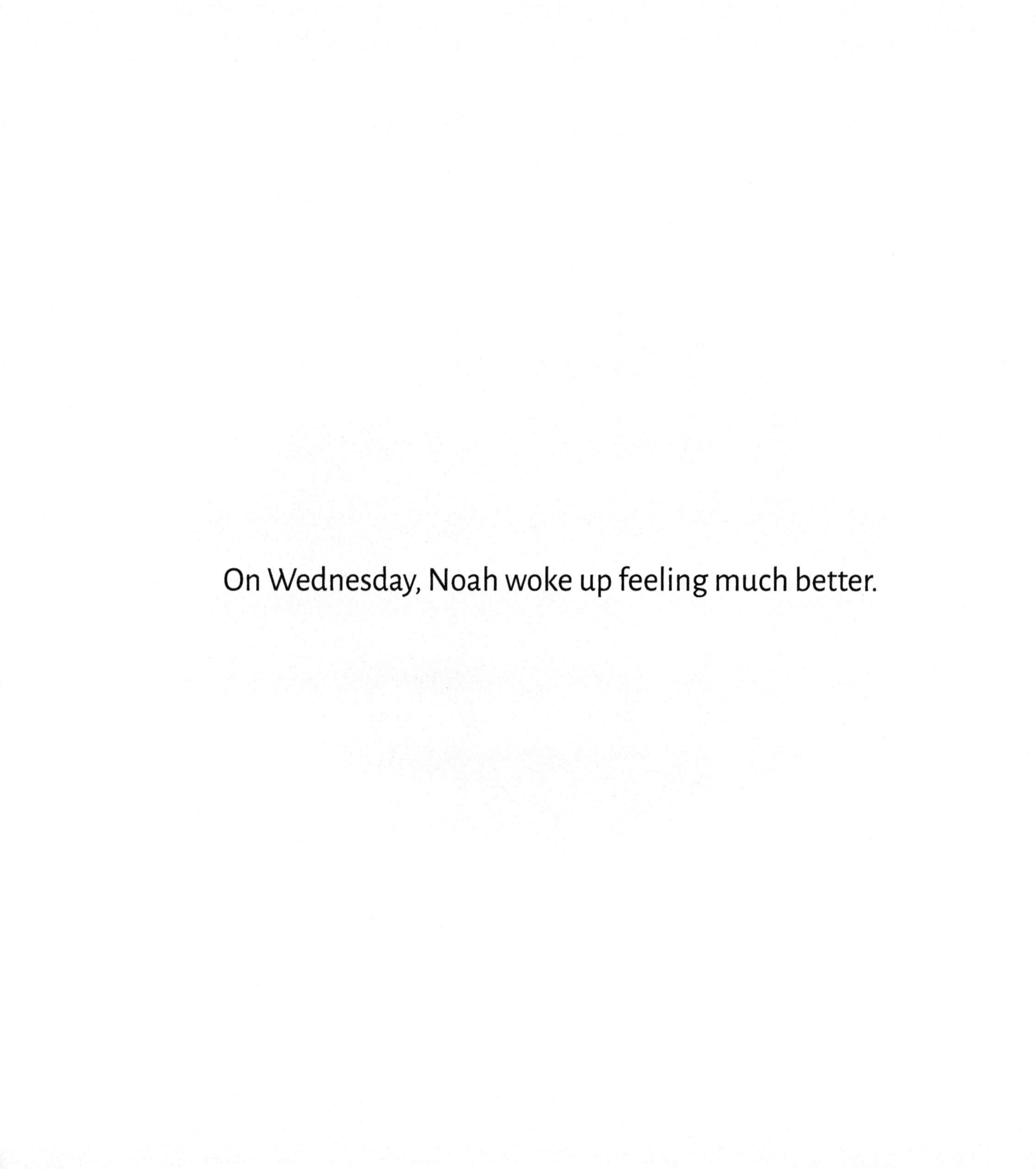

On Wednesday, Noah woke up feeling much better.

“Hello!” he greeted his boss Norbert.

“Harrumph,” said Norbert, narrowing his eyes.

“You look just fine to me.”

“Today is not yesterday,” said Noah meekly.

“How was the movie?” Noah asked Nikki at lunchtime.

“You'd know if you came,” said Nikki.

“Anyway, you look the same as yesterday.”

“Today is not yesterday,” said Noah,

but Nikki had already swum away.

On his way home, Noah called his sister.

"Hello, Nina!" he said.

"I can't just talk whenever you feel like it," said Nina crossly.

"And what was that all about yesterday?

You sound just fine to me."

“Today is not yesterday,” said Noah,

starting to sniff.

That night Noah picked at his dinner for a while before going to bed feeling lonely.

“That Noah!” grumbled Norbert to his wife Nancy over dinner.

“Trying to get out of work!”

“Wasn't Noah the one who worked late all last month
to finish the big electric eel project?”
Nancy reminded him.

“Harrumph,” said Norbert,
but he stopped scowling as he remembered
how well the project had turned out.

"That Noah," said Nikki to her friend Ned.

"You can never rely on him."

"Wasn't Noah the one who brought over a movie when you were sick on your birthday?" said Ned.

Nikki smiled, remembering how they laughed together

over *Penguin Bloopers* 2.

"That brother of mine," Nina thought to herself,

"so self-centered!"

Just then she caught sight of the photos on her refrigerator.

Right in the center was a picture of Noah,

teaching her two little sons to dance.

CLICK
WHISTLE

On Thursday, Noah woke up feeling anxious.

When Noah got to work,

his boss Norbert greeted him with a smile.

“But yesterday you were disappointed with me,” said Noah.

“Today is not yesterday,” said Norbert, looking embarrassed.

He patted Noah on the back.

“I value your work.

That shouldn't change when you don't feel well.”

At lunch,

Nikki waved to him to come and sit next to her.

"But yesterday you were upset with me," said Noah.

“Today is not yesterday,” said Nikki, looking ashamed.

“I value our friendship.

That shouldn't change when you don't feel well.

Here, I brought you this!” Nikki handed him a squid cupcake.

That evening,

Nina brought Noah his favorite fish casserole for dinner.

"But yesterday you were annoyed with me," said Noah.

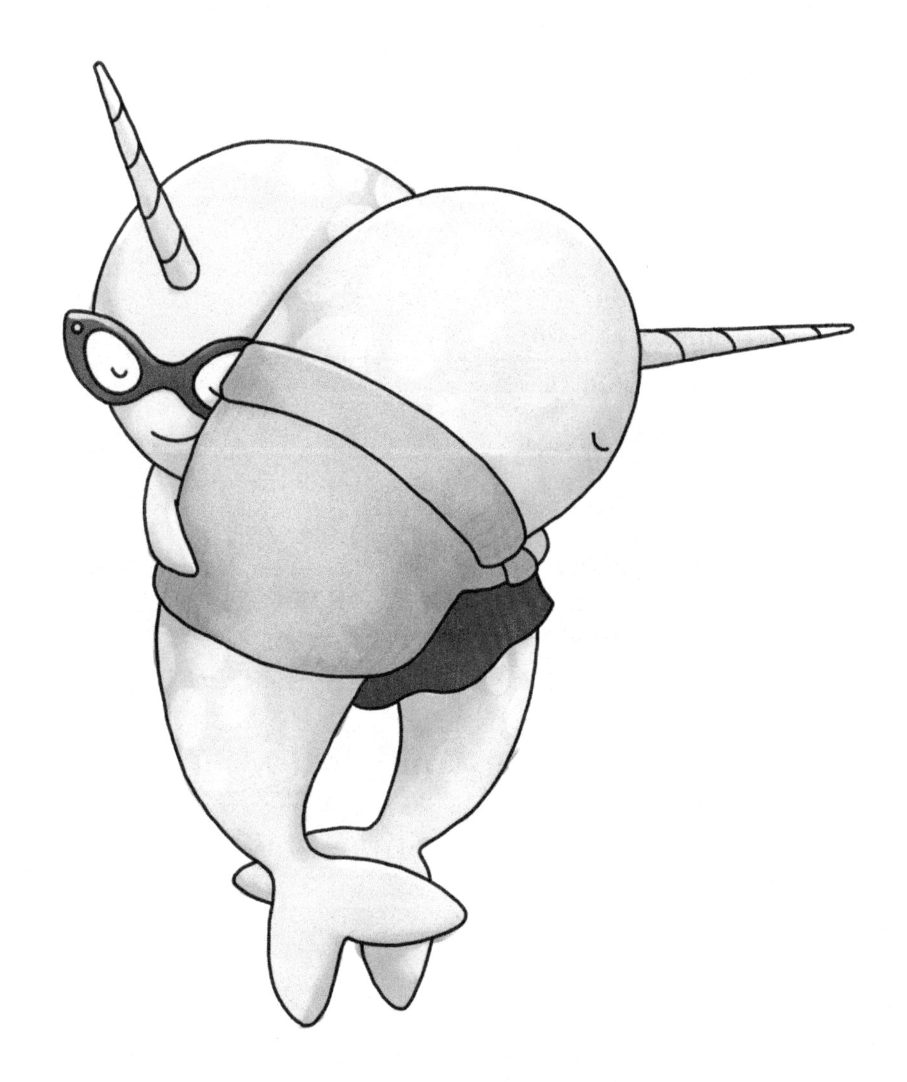

“Today is not yesterday!” Nina declared.

“You are my family.

That doesn't change when you don't feel well.”

And she gave her brother a big hug.

That night, Noah lay in bed thinking.

He didn't know how he would feel when he woke up on Friday,

but he did know that no matter what, he had his friends.

SQUID

Judith Klausner *is a migrainey land mammal from Somerville, Massachusetts. She channels her experience of invisible disability (and everything else) into her creative endeavors. She often makes art using unusual materials from her surroundings and plays with her food both recreationally and professionally. When not creating works of art, she likes to throw fancy dress tea parties. Seeing a lack of characters like herself in picture books, Judith set to work contributing to filling this void, and she hopes that Noah will help other disabled folks of all ages feel less isolated.*

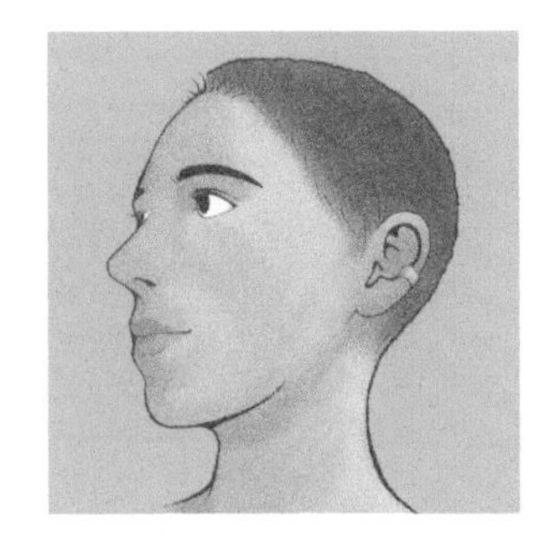

Sarah Gould *is a designer of many things, including games, landscapes, stories, and art. She has grand ambitions to make the world a better place by creating occasionally useful things, but she mostly spends her time noodling, doodling, and trying to understand the full weirdness of human beings. When she's not at work, she can be found tending her blueberry patch at her little house (that she designed!) in a quiet corner of Seattle, WA, or doing some urban hiking on the way to ice cream.*

CPSIA information can be obtained
at www.ICGtesting.com
Printed in the USA
LVOW06*1001070917
547877LV00024B/99/P

9 780999 008423